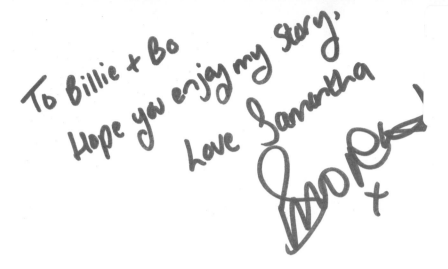

To Billie + Bo
Hope you enjoy my story.
Love Samantha

Samantha lives in County Durham and has been a nurse for over 10 years. She worked as a district nurse and then went on to become a nurse specialist caring for patients following life-changing surgery. She loves working as part of a team and is extremely proud of her profession. Samantha started writing children's stories at the age of 19 but only found the confidence to pursue this dream once she became a mother, which she says is her greatest achievement.

THIS IS HOW WE KISS

GOOD NIGHT

SAMANTHA MORLAND

AUSTIN MACAULEY PUBLISHERS™

LONDON • CAMBRIDGE • NEW YORK • SHARJAH

A CIP catalogue record for this title is available from the British Library.

ISBN 9781788483612 (Paperback)
ISBN 9781528964234 (ePub e-book)

www.austinmacauley.com

First Published (2020)
Austin Macauley Publishers Ltd
25 Canada Square
Canary Wharf
London
E14 5LQ

For my darling daughter, Effie.

"It's nearly time for goodnight kisses,"
said Effie's mummy.
Effie began to wonder if everyone got a
goodnight kiss before bedtime,
so she asked her mummy as they climbed
the stairs together.

"Mummy, does everyone get a goodnight kiss before they go to bed?"
"Well, of course, my darling, but we don't all kiss goodnight the same way," said her mummy.
"How do fairies kiss goodnight?" asked Effie.
"Fairies blow their fairy dust to each other, so it tickles their lips," said her mummy.

Effie thought about this and giggled.
Effie was brushing her teeth with her
dinosaur toothbrush. "What about dinosaurs,
how do they kiss goodnight?"

"Dinosaurs give each other big, sloppy goodnight licks with their huge tongues."
Effie thought about this and gave her mummy a toothpaste smile.

Effie was holding her favourite teddy bear while her mummy brushed her hair. "How do teddy bears kiss goodnight?" she asked.

"Teddy bears do cheek-to-cheek kisses, like this," she took the teddy bear and kissed them on one cheek and then the other.

Effie smiled and kissed her teddy bear
on the cheeks too.
"How do unicorns kiss goodnight?" she asked
while turning her unicorn nightlight on.

"Goodnight,
my darling."

Effie smiled her biggest smile, "I'm pleased everyone gets a goodnight kiss," she said. Effie's mummy tucked her up in bed, leaned towards her and whispered, "And this is how we kiss goodnight." Effie and her mummy began rubbing the tips of their noses together and both began to laugh.

"Butterflies flutter their wings together like this," Effie's mummy made a pair of wings with her hands. Effie did the same and they began
to flutter their hands together.

Effie looked around at her pretty butterfly wallpaper. "What about butterflies?" she yawned.

"What about tigers?" Effie asked,
climbing into bed.
"Tigers bow their heads together like this,"
her mummy touched Effie's head
with her head
and Effie let out a giggle.

"Unicorns press their magical horns together until they glow beautiful colours like your nightlight," said her mummy.